This Little Tiger book belongs to:

For Cameron
L.J.

For Peter John
J.C.

LITTLE TIGER PRESS
An imprint of Magi Publications
1 The Coda Centre, 189 Munster Road, London SW6 6AW
www.littletigerpress.com

First published in Great Britain 1997
This edition published in 1997

Printed in China

ISBN 1 84506 429 1

2 4 6 8 10 9 7 5 3

Penny and Pup

Linda Jennings
illustrated by Jane Chapman

LITTLE TIGER PRESS
London

On the first night in her new home Penny had whined and howled and scratched at the door. So her family gave her Pup to be her friend. Pup was all squashy and floppy and he lived in Penny's basket. She chewed and loved him to bits.

One day Penny and Pup went out into the garden.
Henry the cat was sitting in the yard.
"Hello, Penny," said Henry. "Where are you going?"
Penny put Pup down and gave him a little lick.
"For a walk," said Penny. "Just Pup and me."
"Can I come too?" asked Henry.
"Pup only wants *me* for a friend," she said.
"Sorry."

And, picking Pup
up again, she trotted
down the path.

By the back gate Betsy the
rabbit was sitting in her hutch.
"Penny!" she cried out to her. "Come and talk
to me! It's very boring, all on my own in here."
"Pup doesn't want to stop to talk. We're going
for a walk, just Pup and me," said Penny. "Sorry."

And off she went, with
Pup's long arms and legs
trailing behind her.

On the edge of the
lawn sat Matt the fox cub.
“Come and play with me!” he barked.
“Pup doesn’t like playing with foxes,”
said Penny. “We’re going for a walk,
just Pup and me. Sorry.”

Penny turned her back on Matt and walked with Pup across the lawn to the garden shed.

Under the shed was a big space.
Penny put Pup down gently and sniffed.
It smelled exciting under there, like mice
and old bones.

“We’ll go exploring, Pup and me,” said Penny and, pushing Pup in front of her with her nose, she squeezed her head under the shed.

Penny tried to follow Pup, but she was too big. She wriggled and squeezed and squeezed and wriggled, but she couldn't fit into the space.
"Pup, Pup!" she called, but of course Pup said nothing. Penny tried to pull Pup out again, but she couldn't reach him.
She couldn't even *see* him.

Penny sat down and cried.
What would she do without Pup?
And what would Pup do without *her*?

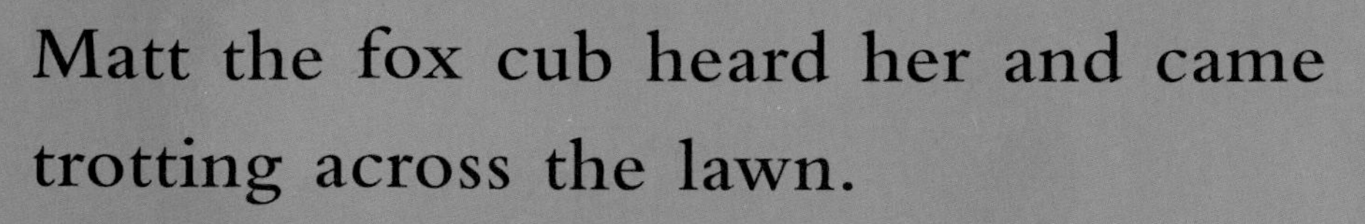

Matt the fox cub heard her and came
trotting across the lawn.
"I'll help you," he said. But though Matt
pushed and squeezed and squeezed and
pushed, he couldn't reach Pup either.

Henry the cat was sitting
on the fence and he saw
Matt trying to rescue Pup.
"*I'll* help you," he said.
But Henry was a fat cat and
he couldn't even squeeze
his *head* under the shed.

Along bounced Betsy the rabbit.
She was feeling happy because she had
managed to escape from her hutch.
"*I'll* help you," she said. And because Betsy
was a small rabbit she was able to wriggle
and squeeze and squeeze and wriggle under
the shed – but Pup wasn't there any more!

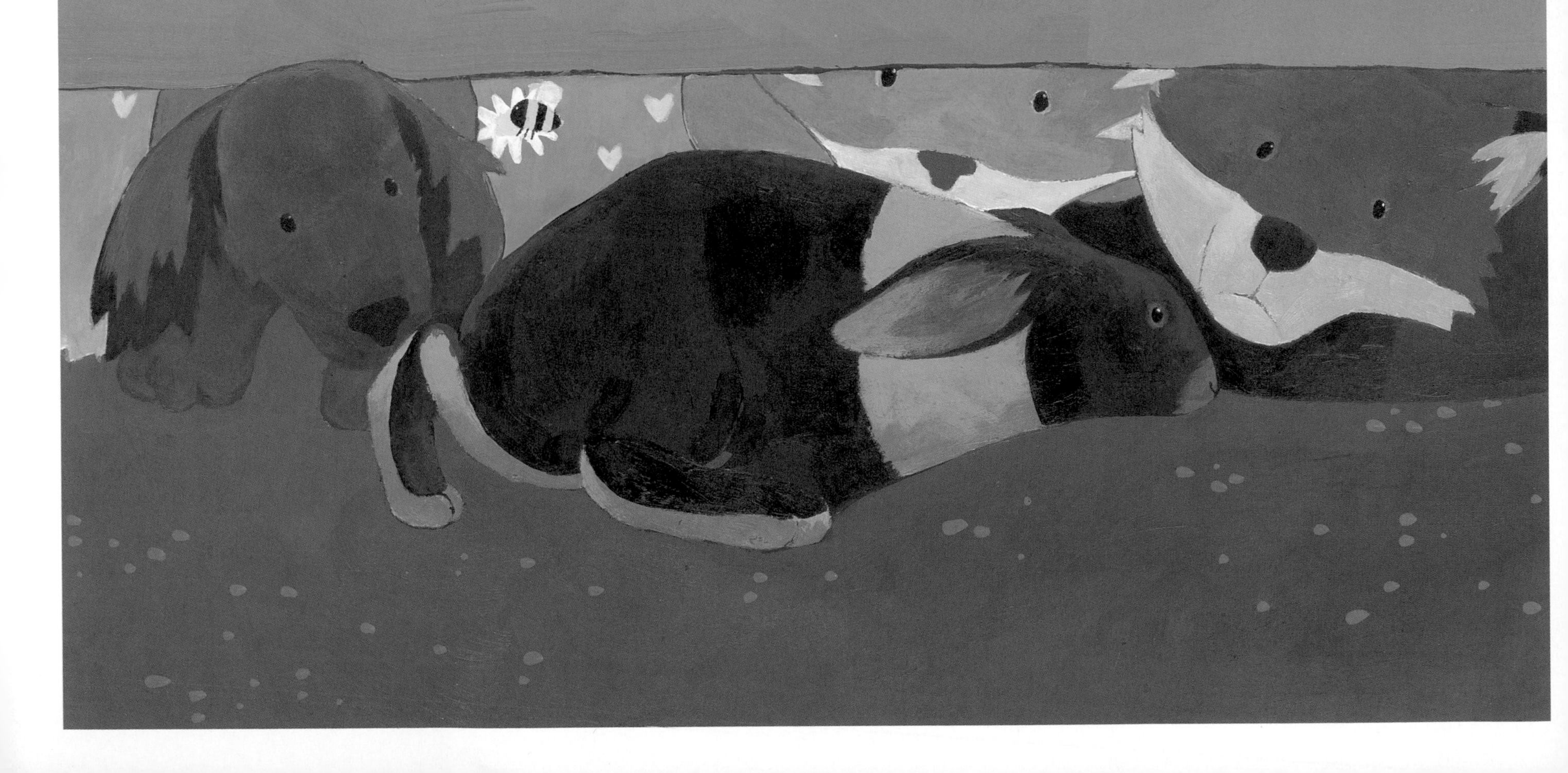

Matt and Henry and Betsy all helped
Penny to look for Pup.
They looked behind the shed.
They looked in the flower beds.
They even looked in the pond,
just in case Pup had fallen in.
But Pup wasn't anywhere to be found.
And then suddenly . . .

. . . there he was!
Pup was lying in the hedge where a family of mice had dragged him. The mice were all curled up in Pup's long dangly arms, fast asleep.

Penny looked at Pup and she looked at the mice.
It seemed a pity to disturb them.
“Come and play with us instead!” mieowed Henry.
“Yes, do!” cried Matt and Betsy together.
“You don’t mind, do you, Pup?” asked Penny,
but Pup said nothing.

"All right, I *will* play with you," said Penny and she raced and chased and chased and raced all around the garden with her new friends. Penny was having such fun that she forgot about Pup.

When it was teatime Penny remembered poor old Pup lying in the hedge and went back to fetch him.

The baby mice were still
asleep, but Mother Mouse was awake.
"May we borrow your Pup?" she asked Penny.
"He makes such a lovely bed for my babies."
Pup looked very happy with the little mice
in his arms.

“They need Pup more than I do,” thought Penny. “Now I have real friends of my own.”
“Yes, you can have Pup,” Penny said to Mother Mouse. “I don’t think I need him any more.”

More fantastic books from Little Tiger Press

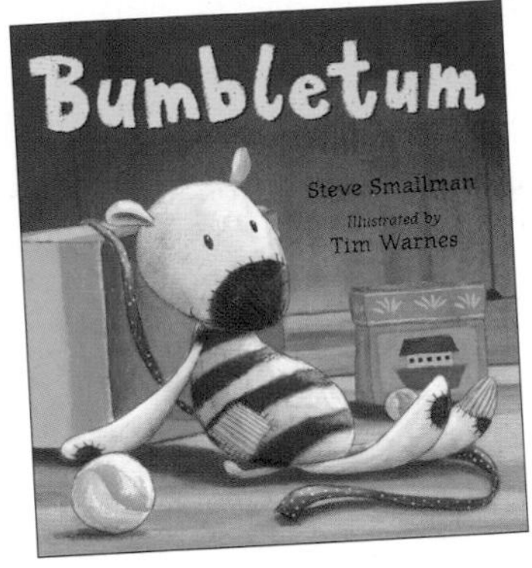

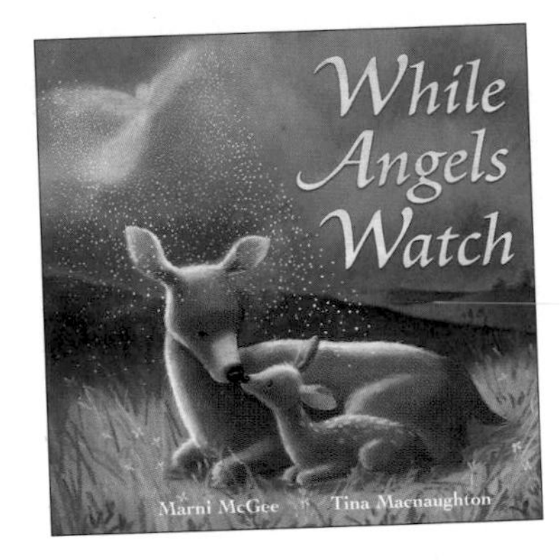

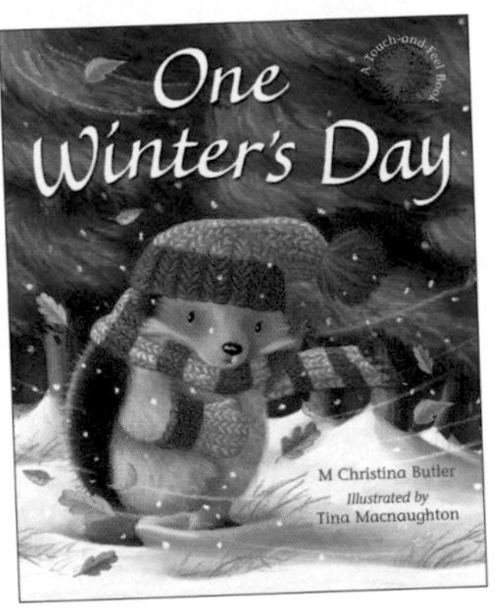

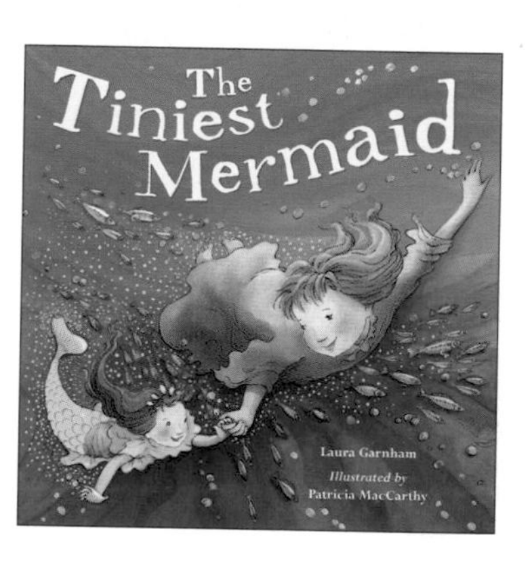

For information regarding any of the above titles
or for our catalogue, please contact us:

Little Tiger Press, 1 The Coda Centre,
189 Munster Road, London SW6 6AW, UK
Tel: 020 7385 6333 Fax: 020 7385 7333
E-mail: info@littletiger.co.uk
www.littletigerpress.com